DOG DIARIES

DASH

DOG DIARIES

DOG DIARIES

DASH

BY KATE KLIMO • ILLUSTRATED BY TIM JESSELL

RANDOM HOUSE 🏠 NEW YORK

The author and editor would like to thank Karin J. Goldstein,
Robert Charlebois, Peter Arenstam, and Denise Lebica,
Plimoth Plantation, for their assistance in the preparation of this book.

Text copyright © 2014 by Kate Klimo
Cover art and interior illustrations copyright © 2014 by Tim Jessell
Photographs courtesy of Picture Collection, the New York Public Library, Astor, Lenox and
Tilden Foundations, p. ix; © Persley Photographics/Flickr/Getty Images, p. 140.

Visit us on the Web! randomhouse.com/kids

Educators and librarians, for a variety of teaching tools, visit us at
RHTeachersLibrarians.com

Library of Congress Cataloging-in-Publication Data
Klimo, Kate.
Dash / by Kate Klimo ; illustrated by Tim Jessell. — First edition.
pages cm. — (Dog diaries ; #5)
Summary: "An English Springer spaniel's tale of the *Mayflower* voyage and the first
Thanksgiving at Plymouth Colony." —Provided by publisher.
ISBN 978-0-385-37338-8 (trade) — ISBN 978-0-385-37339-5 (lib. bdg.) —
ISBN 978-0-385-37340-1 (ebook)
1. English springer spaniels—Juvenile fiction. [1. English springer spaniels—Fiction.
2. Dogs—Fiction. 3. Pilgrims (New Plymouth Colony)—Fiction. 4. Mayflower (Ship)—
Fiction. 5. Thanksgiving Day—Fiction. 6. Plymouth (Mass.)—History—17th century—
Fiction.] I. Jessell, Tim, illustrator. II. Title.
PZ10.3.K686 Das 2014 [Fic]—dc23 2013032531

Printed in the United States of America

10 9 8

First Edition

For Alice Jonaitis, who knows from dogs
—K.K.

To the "can-do" spirit of Dash
—T.J.

CONTENTS

The *Mayflower* at sea

THE DASHING ONE

An angry ocean has all but swallowed up the good ship *Mayflower.* For days, it has been lashed by rains and tossed by waves. The deck teeters beneath my feet. I claw my way upward one moment, only to come slipping and sliding down the next. The ship lurches, and I tumble head over tail. I stand up and shake myself hard. I am soaked to the skin. My head reels! This is no life for a simple hunting dog.

The three seamen who hang above me in the

rigging look down and laugh, as if I am offering up an entertainment. It is true that I am given to antics. But not this day.

"Yon spaniel is quite the little jester!" one of them shouts to the others above the wind.

"Nay, he has yet to find his sea legs!" the second shouts back.

"Is *that* what he's looking for?" the third adds with a harsh laugh. "I thought he was looking for landfall!"

"He'll have to look a good deal harder for that!" the first bellows. "We are weeks behind on this voyage! It will be winter before we drop anchor!"

"*If* ever we drop anchor!" the second shouts. "'Tis a punishing sea we cross."

"How now? You sound as fearful as the Saints," the third sailor jeers.

My floppy ears twitch. The Saints are *my* people.

They are sailing on this ship to a Distant Shore, where they seek Freedom to Worship God. I do not understand worshipping God. But Freedom I do understand.

Freedom for me is a marsh on a misty morn. I am zigzagging through the reeds, seeking game fowl. I dash forward and pounce as wings explode around me. I hunker down. Behind me, John Goodman lifts the barrel of his musket and fires. Then I dash forward once again to find the fallen one. I take it ever so gently into my mouth and run back to John Goodman.

"Hup," he says.

I sit and stay. I lift my head and offer up my gift. He takes it from me.

"Ah! The softest mouth of any dog in England!" he says as he strokes my head.

As tasty as I know the bird to be, my teeth

never pierce it. Any bird I retrieve is fit for the table. As my reward later, John Goodman will toss the skin and bones to me. And are not skin and bones the best parts?

My name is Dash. I am a springer spaniel. And dashing after game fowl is what I was born and bred to do.

The passengers seldom venture up on deck, but calls of nature and a hankering for fresh air bring me up here at least twice a day. I try not to let the seabirds spoil my outing. They do not smell sweet like woodcocks. They reek of fish guts. The ship rocks too hard for them to find a perch. Instead, they wheel overhead, screeching and mocking me, just like the seamen.

Where, I wonder, is my Furry Fellow, she who comes to the name of Mercy? I have not seen her since rough seas set in three nights ago. She is huge and magnificent, the breed of dog that men call mastiff. Her kind was bred for war. In London Town, she tells me—where our good master, John Goodman, found her—she fought bears for the amusement of the crowds. On her chest are scars left by their claws. Happily, her bear-fighting days are behind her. Her job now is to guard John Goodman, a job that she does very well.

I know she is aboard the *Mayflower* somewhere, but I cannot find her. The wind snatches her scent away before I can home in on it. Nor have I been able to locate John Goodman himself.

My one consolation has been the company of the young lads and lass, the brothers Love Brewster and Wrestling Brewster and their friend Remember Allerton. They while away the time belowdecks playing at games they call Hickety-Hackety and Leapfrog and Nine Men's Morris. They play quietly with voices hushed. They do not want to stir the wrath of the seamen or disturb the passengers who are fearful of or sickened by the voyage.

Suddenly, something strikes me in the head. A moldy boot! Its owner limps up behind me. "Got you!" he says with a cruel snicker.

It is that young rascal Francis Billington! He is forever sneaking up on me. What with climbing the masts and filching from the stores, he is no one's favorite. I growl but do not snap at him. I must harm no passenger lest I be pitched into the sea. Francis retrieves his boot and ducks behind a barrel just as the cabin door blows wide open.

"There you are, Dash!"

I turn and yelp with joy. My friends! The lads and lass crowd the doorway. I fly to them.

Save me from that rogue Billington! I cry.

"Come belowdecks, before we lose you to the

sea," says the younger brother, Wrestling. He grabs my collar and drags me down the steps. On the gun deck below, it is dark, smelling of sickness and fear. But these young ones will have no part in it. Nor do they ever have anything but a kind word for me—which is more than I can say for that bad, bad Billington boy!

Love kneels before me and whispers, "We are playing at Pirates. We've just boarded this fair ship."

"And we're plundering her for treasure!" adds Remember.

Their eyes gleam. I don't understand the game, but I feel their excitement and wag what is left of my tail. Once it was long, but John Goodman docked it after I broke it in a thicket, chasing a pheasant.

For the moment, I forget John Goodman and

Mercy. I follow the children as they creep down the aisle. Through the thin walls, I hear the passengers groaning. We stop and peer into each narrow room. Lying on straw mats or lumpy mattresses, the people look pale and drawn. Not all are Saints. Some are Strangers. Like pirates, the Strangers seek treasure and prizes. All the passengers are weary of and sickened by this voyage.

We come upon the Billington cabin. Have I said that Francis Billington has a brother? He does, and he is no less of a ne'er-do-well. He lies sprawled in a pile of rags, idly slapping a hank of rope against his palm. When he sees us, he snarls, "Begone before I take my whip to you!"

I pity Mistress Billington, to have two such sorry boys. Her husband is no better. The Billingtons are Strangers, but they stand apart from Saints and Strangers both. The way some dogs are driven from the pack because they are mangy or sly, this family is outcast.

I curl my lip at John Billington and growl to let him know that I have no fear of him or his rope.

Love grabs ahold of my collar and yanks me away. "There is no gold to be found here," he says.

Suddenly, from down the aisle, I hear a scratchy cry. I break loose and run ahead to another cabin. There, on a mattress, Mistress Elizabeth lies. Her brood surrounds her: Constance, Giles, and Damaris. In her arms, something white and pink and wrapped in a blanket wriggles. The woman smiles when she sees me and sits up.

"Hello, Dash!" she says. "Have you come to welcome the newest passenger?"

I race over and hurl myself at the mattress. Love, Wrestling, and Remember approach shyly behind me. They look down on the wriggling thing in her

arms. What a tiny, wrinkled face it has!

Remember's breath catches in her throat. "That is treasure, indeed!" says she.

"Pshaw!" says Wrestling, backing off. "It's only a newborn babe."

"I have named him Oceanus," says the proud mother.

"A fitting name for a pirate," says Love. "Good health to you and your babe, Mistress Hopkins."

"Come away, mates," says Wrestling from the

entryway. "Let us not forget the pirate treasure."

"Do you feel it?" Love says when we are once again in the aisle.

The lad and lass stare at him, as do I.

"The *Mayflower* has ceased to lurch," says Love with a wide smile. "The seas have grown calm. Now all we need is the pirate treasure and our good fortune will be complete."

"I have an idea!" says Wrestling, raising a finger. "Perhaps the treasure lies below us in the hold!"

Remember's eyes are wide. "But we cannot go down there, Wrestling," she says. "Master Jones will clap us in irons."

"Master Jones need never know," says Love with a careless toss of his head.

They tiptoe back down the aisle toward the amidships hatch. All around us lie piles of planks. They are the parts of the passengers' shallop. It is a wooden sailboat they will put together when we find Safe Harbor. Love looks fore and aft, then slowly lifts the hatch.

My nostrils twitch. Wafting up from down below are the scents of pork fat and dried beef and oats and fruits. I also detect rats. In the first days at sea, I brought many a rat to John Goodman. Without so much as a thank-thee, he took them by the tail and flung them overboard into the sea. Oh! The waste!

We run down the steep stairway into the gloom. Barrels and boxes and crates of food are stacked everywhere.

All at once, I freeze and lift my nose. I pick up a scent, sharp and clear. The scent has a shape—two shapes, in fact. They are the beloved shapes of my master, John Goodman, and my Furry Fellow, Mercy!

2

PUKE STOCKINGS

"Do you see?" says Wrestling. "I knew Dash had a nose for gold."

I am off, zigzagging through the stacks of barrels and boxes, the lads and lass hard at my heels.

And there he is! My master!

He is lying on the bare deck next to a bucket. His face is pale and damp with sweat. Mercy lies belly down next to him, her body as long as his. She lifts her head and casts me a look. With her

13

sagging jowls and great golden eyes, my Furry Fellow always looks a bit woeful, but today she seems more so.

Hello, my little friend, says she.

I pounce upon her and fasten my mouth around her jaw. *Where have you been, you silly dog? I have looked all over the ship for you! Why are you hiding down here?*

She answers as we tussle. *John Goodman came here to nurse his sickness. I could not leave him alone.*

"Please, dogs!" John Goodman rasps. "No horsing around! I am sick unto death, I tell you!"

He rolls over and gags.

I stop playing and watch as my master seems to wring his very guts out into the bucket.

I see how it is, I say grimly.

Mercy licks his face gently.

The lads and lass have backed away, disappointed that I have led them not to treasure but to just one more sickly passenger.

I remain with my master. The children understand that my loyalty is to him. I say to Mercy, *It is not good for him to be down here in the dank hold. He needs to be up on deck, in the fresh air.*

Mercy cocks her noble head. *Do you think so?* she says. Everything about Mercy is big, except perhaps her brain. She may not be the smartest dog I have ever met, but her courage is unmatched.

The three pirates are already clambering up the steps.

I let out a lively yip. *Come along, John Goodman, if you know what is good for you!*

John Goodman groans, "Go away and let me be, Dash!"

I bark at Mercy. *Make him come!*

Mercy rises to her full height and shakes herself

from head to tail. It is as if a great brown rug is being beaten out. Bits of dust and fur fly all about. I sneeze. When the cloud settles, she grabs John Goodman's sleeve in her teeth and pulls at him. Again, he groans.

"Not you too, girl!"

Mercy keeps at it until John Goodman gives up. He stands, reeling, his hand braced on a stack of crates. Gradually, he steadies himself.

"The ship has stopped pitching!" he says.

Leaning on Mercy, with me leading, John Goodman makes his way to the upper deck.

The clouds have rolled away, and the sun beams down. John Goodman takes in the fresh air, like a thirsty man gulping water. Then he closes his eyes and basks. Gradually, the pink returns to his cheeks. Mercy looks on, wagging her long, furry spike of a tail.

Do you see what I mean? I say to her.

She gives out a friendly growl. *Dash! You have brains enough for the both of us. Come here!*

I run over. What a lot of dog she is! She is so tall I can fit my body beneath her belly with room to spare. Then I spy a gull perched in the rigging of the mainsail.

Catch me if you can! it says with a sneer.

I scramble out from under Mercy and make a mad run for the gull. I send it flapping and squawking back to the sky.

You're lucky I don't have wings! I bark and bark.

John Goodman holds his belly and laughs. It is the first time I have heard him make such a happy sound since we set sail from England.

"That's my saucy little springer!" he says. "When we get to the Distant Shore, there will be birds aplenty for you to dash after."

* * *

But the fair weather is too good to last. The following day, dark clouds again boil up and hide the sun. Winds howl. Rains pelt down endlessly and soak everyone and everything on board. Our firewood is too wet to burn. Teeth chatter. Food rots in the hold. Passengers nibble on crusts and scraps and drink water not even fit for a dog. People say that we dogs stink, but there is nothing to match the stench of these miserable, unwashed voyagers.

Many, like John Goodman, continue to be seasick. They lean on the rails and heave up into the foamy waters. The seamen look on in disgust. They call the passengers *puke stockings.* Mercy and I are *useless curs* and *rag mops* worthy only to swab the deck. We steer clear of the seamen and dodge their boot heels. Even the passengers have lost their fondness for us. They grumble when John Goodman feeds us from the food stores, so he stops. Mercy and I must fend for ourselves. The rats are as skinny as we are, but at least they are fresh. We enjoy the meat but not the fleas that leap from their cold bodies onto our warm ones. The fleas are like passengers of a sinking ship crowding onto a boat. We scratch and bite until our hides are raw.

As if all this were not bad enough, one day a mighty wind splits the main beam with a loud crack. The sailors groan. The passengers emerge from below with a Screw Thing. With it they clamp the broken beam, then mend it. The seamen are grudging in their thanks. Meanwhile, Death takes one of the passengers. A mere child. His small body is tossed into the sea.

"That's one less puke stocking," a surly seaman mutters.

One stormy morning, I go up on deck to lift my leg in my usual spot—a heap of coiled rope. I look about before I attend to my business, lest naughty Francis Billington be lurking nearby. I see only the man named John Howland. He seems unsteady on his feet this day. I follow him as he staggers along the deck. Suddenly, the *Mayflower* tilts, and he pitches into the sea! I bark and run back and forth.

Man overboard! I call out until my throat is raw.

I peer through the rails and see him splashing in the water by the side of the ship. He has grabbed on to the end of a trailing rope.

One of the seamen comes over to see why I have set up such a racket. "What now, fleabag?" he asks, making ready to land a kick in my ribs.

Then he hears John Howland gasping down below. He hauls the poor man up, first by rope and then by hook. John Howland lies on deck, spitting and choking. Master Jones, the *Mayflower's* captain, arrives. He bends over and scratches my ear.

"This dog saved your life, John," Master Jones says to the man. "You ought to thank him."

John Howland reaches out a limp hand to me. I lick it. His hand is so salty it makes me thirsty.

After I have finished lifting my leg, I lap up some rainwater that has pooled in a pile of canvas. But even this tastes more of salt than of water. I gag in disgust. Then I feel a sharp tug on my tail. I swing around and very nearly snap. It is Francis Billington!

"Can't catch me, fleabag!" he shouts, and prances out of my reach.

Grrrrrrr.

I turn around and walk away, my nose in the air. I wouldn't chase that boy if he was my own lost tail.

In the days that follow, the Saints spend much time with their hands clasped and their eyes gazing heavenward. Sometimes they sing in woeful voices. On the ship, as on land, the passengers cease all work every so often. It is the Praying Day. On the

Praying Day, neither do we dogs work.

What is praying, and why do they do it? Mercy asks me.

They are begging God to keep them safe, I say, *because they are frightened.*

Safe from what? the big girl asks.

How should I know? Fleas? Mange? Man-eating fish? I really have no idea. These are only guesses. We dogs can only ponder the many strange habits of humans.

What is God? Mercy wonders.

God to them is as John Goodman is to us. He is like a master, or a father, I say to her.

Mercy bends herself in half to reach a flea just above her tail. When she is finished, she unfolds herself and sighs. *When we are on land, John Goodman plays with us. He runs with us and throws sticks for us to fetch and plays Rope War. Does God play like this with the Saints?*

Mercy is a good soul, but sometimes she asks too many questions. I am saved from having to provide an answer by a shout from high in the rigging.

Everyone rushes up from below and crowds onto the deck. The entire ship tilts toward the water. I scramble to keep from sliding overboard. Above me, necks crane and eyes blink in disbelief. Some weep. Others fall to their knees and call out

thanks to God. Mercy and I wonder at all the excitement. Then our twitching noses tell us.

Deer, says Mercy.

Birds of the field, say I.

The Distant Shore! At long last.

Mercy draws herself to her full height and puffs
out her mighty chest. *It is time for us dogs to go to
work,* she says.

But not yet, for the *Mayflower* sails on, in
search of calmer waters. Finally, we draw nearer to

the shore. The anchor drops with a loud splash.

The passengers send up a loud "huzzah!"

Mercy and I leap about and bark joyfully. Then we stop and look around in puzzlement.

We have arrived, and yet no one leaves the ship. Around us, voices rise in argument. Some want to climb into the longboat and row ashore. Others say we are not meant to land here. Our destination lies farther south, they argue. The seamen mutter to each other. "One harbor is the same as any other."

In a loud, ringing voice, Master Jones puts an end to all argument with a stern look. "Winter is coming. It is too dangerous for us to sail southward. Captain Standish will head up a landing party. We will look for our new home here."

Captain Standish is a soldier hired by the passengers. He is a runt of a man. The seamen call him Captain Shrimp, but I am not fooled by his size. Just as I am small but strong and clever and quick, so is Captain Myles Standish. As Master Jones led us on board the *Mayflower*, so Captain Standish will now lead us onto this shore.

Menfolk pile into the captain's cabin. The women and children are left to themselves. The women fold their arms and stare toward the beach, where waves explode against the rocks.

"It is a savage land. Even the waves are cruel," says Mistress Elizabeth, the mother of Oceanus.

Love and Wrestling and Remember play with us on deck, but their ears, like ours, are cocked toward the cabin, where the voices drone on.

"When will we get off this ship?" says Wrestling.

"Mother said this morning that it has been sixty-six days since her feet touched land," Love adds.

"My father says we cannot go ashore until the grown folk have made a compact," Remember explains.

"How long does it take to make a compact?" Wrestling says.

"And what *is* a compact, anyway?" Love asks.

"It is a written agreement," says Remember gravely. "One that sets down the rules for how we will behave in the new land."

"Well, I wish they would make faster work of it," Wrestling grumbles.

I watch the children's faces and try to make out what this all means. Are we leaving the ship? Are we staying on board forever? At present, we are fetching sticks. First Mercy gets the stick. I make to take it from her. We play at War, each holding one end of the stick in our teeth. We tug and growl. We glare. Mercy lets me have the stick and

I stagger backward under its weight. The children laugh at our antics. I run up to Remember and she says, "Hup."

I sit and stay and offer up the stick.

"A fine bird you have fetched," she says, wiping the slime from the stick onto her apron.

Then she flings the stick, and the game starts all over again. If I cannot work, I will gladly play.

Finally, the men emerge from the cabin. They clap each other on the backs.

"They have finished the compact!" Remember says.

Can we go ashore now? Mercy asks, tail thumping the rail.

ON THE DISTANT SHORE

The next day being the Praying Day, we remain on board. On Praying Day, the children must join in the prayers. Mercy and I wait, tongues out, lapping up all the new scents, eager to set our paws upon this strange, new land.

The following morning, John Goodman comes to fetch us as we romp on deck with the lads and lass.

"Can you spare us your furry playmates?" John

Goodman says to the children. "The dogs are needed ashore with the landing party."

Mercy and I fall to our haunches and wait for our orders.

"Can we come, too?" Love asks.

"Not yet," says John Goodman. "First, Standish must find a Safe Harbor for us to make our new home. The dogs will help."

Remember throws her arms around Mercy. "Find us a good home, girl," she says.

Wrestling kneels and raps me fondly on the nose. "Look before you leap, Dash."

Francis Billington hovers nearby. He sneers. "They will not let you go ashore, but I am going."

Francis starts to climb into the longboat. But his brother, John, falls upon him and boxes his ear. "You cannot go ashore. You are too young and useless!"

Rubbing his reddened ear, Francis skulks off. There are tears in his eyes. In that moment, I see that he is more to be pitied than loathed. If I had a brother who beat me about the ears, I would be a cur unfit for polite company, too.

Then John lifts a leg to climb into the boat. A passenger swoops down upon him, picks him up by the scruff of the neck, and tosses him aside. "Remain on board and stay out of trouble!"

John Billington backs off and mutters darkly, "I hope you get eaten by bears."

"What did you say?" The passenger turns on him, lifting a warning hand.

"Good luck in all your affairs," says John Billington with a false smile, before going belowdecks.

Now John Goodman waves a hand toward the longboat, which is lashed to the deck. "Jump in, my friends," he says to Mercy and me.

We stare at the boat and wag our tails. Unlike the brothers Billington, we are not so eager to climb aboard.

"Go on, now!" John Goodman says sternly when we hesitate.

First Mercy and then I scramble into the longboat.

Now what? Mercy whines.

We are thankful when our master climbs in after us. "Easy, dogs," he says. He tries to sound calm, but his hand on my collar trembles. We huddle next to our master. As frightened as we ourselves are, we will protect him.

Suddenly, the boat rises up into the air and sways. Mercy falls onto her back.

Seamen pulling on ropes are causing the boat to rise up into the air.

Mercy rights herself and barks at them: *Stop*

this instant! Say, what do you think you're doing?

They enjoy a good laugh at my big girl's expense and hoist the boat yet higher. The boat swings out over the side of the ship. We are hanging in midair!

Whatever will become of us? Mercy moans.

Then the seamen lower the boat until it rests on the water. There it sits, rocking gently as, one by one, more men climb down a rope from the ship into the boat. It wobbles as each settles himself.

Among the men are William Bradford, Stephen Hopkins, and John Tilley—good men, all. They wear armor and carry muskets and axes and swords. Mercy and I will be very busy protecting them.

Captain Standish sits in the bow, his eyes fierce. The men dip the oars in the water and row toward the shore. The waves lift us high and higher. I hear

Mercy whimper. The men ship their oars. Wave after wave urges the boat ever closer to the land.

The shore looks empty and windswept. There are no buildings, no smoke, no horses, no wagons. No people! Where are the people? Crowds of people saw us off in England. Is there not one person here to greet us?

Two of the men leap into the shallows to pull the boat up onto the sand. I can wait no longer. I shake free of my master's grasp and leap overboard into the surf.

Oh! It is so very cold! I gasp.

Don't leave me, Dash! Mercy pleads.

Mercy leaps after me, making a huge splash. We hold our heads above the water and paddle until we feel the sand beneath our feet. Together we run until we are far up onto the loose sand, which is warm and so dry! Everything aboard that ship has been wet and cold for as long as we can remember. We sink into the sand and roll over onto our backs. We work the sand into our coats, wallowing in the scents of this new land, the better to hide from predators and prey alike.

The men follow us into the water, crying out at the cold. They stagger onto the shore and fall to their knees. Some kiss the very sand. They send up thanks to God.

And then they are back on their feet, brushing off the sand. They begin chopping and gathering wood. But what is *our* work to be?

"Don't wander off," John Goodman says to us.

As if we would in such a place! We circle about, sniffing out small rodents and birds and deer.

And here is the puzzling thing: we *smell* people, but we do not *see* people.

The shore of England teemed with people of all shapes and sizes, speaking in many tongues. Even in the dead of night, it was a noisy babble. Except for the wind raking the dunes and the waves lashing the shore, this land is quiet and empty.

The fur stands up along Mercy's spine. *I do not like it,* she says.

It is better than being on the ship, say I. Besides, I have my eye on some birds. John Goodman has but to say the word and I will go forth and flush them out.

Beware, birds. Dash has arrived!

The men busy themselves with axes, chopping down small, sweet-smelling trees. Soon, the boat is piled with stacks of fresh-cut wood and dry brush.

John Goodman whistles us in. It is a sweet and familiar sound in a strange place.

"Tonight," he says, rubbing his hands together, "we will have fire on board the *Mayflower* for the first time in weeks."

Fire. We know that word. We love fire, so long as people keep it in its place. We climb into the boat, and the men row us back to the *Mayflower.*

That night, the men build a fine fire smelling of this new land. Mercy and I creep up close to the heat. My coat steams.

"Sleep well, dogs," John Goodman says. "For soon, we will be returning to shore."

Today, the harbor teems with monsters. They are big black creatures that bask and leap and squirt tall spouts of water. Each time one of them swims into view, Wrestling cries out, "Whale!" and all the children run over to the rails to see. One whale floats so near the *Mayflower* that Mercy starts to growl.

Stay away from the children, or I will bite you hard! she says. *Know that I have fought bears.*

I don't think the whale is listening. It seems to me that the whale sleeps.

One of the passengers fetches his musket and fires at the whale. The black giant lets out an angry snort and dives beneath the water. Mercy is disappointed that she will not have a chance to show the whale what she is made of.

The women are rowed ashore to wash clothes. Before she goes, Mistress Elizabeth says to me, "I've a good mind to drag you ashore and give you a bath."

I run away. *Bath* is a bad, bad word.

The next day, we go ashore in three groups. I am with John Goodman and Master Jones. Sadly, Mercy is with Captain Standish and his men. A third group remains on the beach with the big pile of wooden boat parts and the barrel of pegs from the *Mayflower*. They will peg together the pieces of wood to make the shallop.

I do not like being apart from my Furry Fellow. But I say to Mercy, *It is John Goodman's wish. Courage.*

I watch her group march off in a line, armed with muskets and swords. As for me, I tend to what I do best. I hunt ducks and geese in the marshlands near the shore. The ducks and geese here are not so very different from the ones in England. I flush them out. John Goodman shoots them as they rise up into the air. I dash forward and bring back the fallen ones.

"Hup," says John Goodman.

One after another, I offer up enough ducks and geese to make a pretty string of them hanging around John Goodman's neck. He rubs my ears.

When he rejoins the men, they marvel at the birds. John Goodman says, "Did I not tell you that this dog was the very thing we needed?"

I wag my stub of a tail. I am pleased to be of service.

Later, the other group returns. They are quiet and smell of fear.

Mercy is excited and happy. She runs up to me and crouches, hind end in the air. *We saw men on the beach. And guess what? They had a dog with them! One of us! But the men smelled different. They look different, too. Standish calls them savages.*

I knew I smelled people, I say. *They must have been hiding.*

The dog came forward to greet me with hackles raised, with ears flat and lips curled. He was lean and strong. Neither as big as I nor as small as you. "This is my land," said the dog. "What is your business here?" Before I could answer that we are here to stay, so he might as well get used to us, his master whistled him away.

Do you see? I say. Their masters call their dogs with a whistle, just as ours do. How alike we are! Men who know the company of dogs cannot possibly be savages.

Mercy continues with her tale. *The natives and their dog ran into the thick of the woods. We followed, but the sad fact is our men could not keep up. I might have chased after them all night, but our men are weakened by the voyage.*

Darkness falls. The wind is chill. The men have built a fire on the beach. I am glad we are not returning to the ship. Instead of a pitching deck, the land feels solid and sure beneath my feet. The men dress the birds and roast them over the fire. There are scraps aplenty for Mercy and me.

So far, I say to Mercy as I lick the duck grease from my chops, *I am all for this Distant Shore.*

Mercy grins happily as she gnaws the marrow from the knob of a goose's drumstick.

The next morning, I am pleased that I can go with Mercy's group. We are following the tracks of the native party they spied on the beach yesterday. The scent is fresh, and we stay with it until the sun is low in the sky. Suddenly, Mercy and I catch sight of a deer. Off we run!

John Goodman whistles us back, but we are disobedient. It is our nature to run after prey. We see the deer's white tail as it leaps through the woods. We follow it through brush and brambles, the men shouting and wheezing and stumbling after us.

At last, we come to the foot of a hill. The deer has vanished, but now we smell something new. Fresh water! Thirsty from our run, Mercy and I splash into the middle of the pool and lap up the cold, sweet water.

The men soon arrive, weary and grumbling and vexed with us. Then they see the water.

"Thank ye, dogs!" one man cries as he splashes into the pool and scoops up handfuls of water.

The others fall to their knees and drink from cupped hands. The water puts new life into them.

We go with the men as they march in a line back to the shore. There they build up the fire, and we spend our second night in camp within view of the *Mayflower*. As I look out into the harbor, I think I can see Love on deck, waving to us. Mightily tired from the day's adventures, I welcome the fire's warmth.

Alas, Mercy is not permitted to lie by the fire. She must stand guard with the men who watch over our camp. Not wishing to be apart from my Furry Fellow, I nestle down next to her. Each time I awake in the night, I rest easy, knowing that Mercy guards us. Oh, noble beast!

Early the next morning, we are off again. Soon, we come upon a field such as I have run through in England. The crops have been taken and only burnt stubble remains. We follow a narrow path and arrive at a mound of sand with some woven grass mats atop it. The men dig into the sand with shovels. We dogs dig in with paws. Together, we unearth sticks with sharp points and what Bradford calls a Hunting Bow. From the smell of them, I take these to be native weapons.

Then Mercy and I catch a whiff of Death and Decay. We back away from the hole. Mercy's hackles have risen. I whine, *Let's be gone from this place.*

"It is an Indian grave," William Bradford says. "The dogs have the right idea. Best not to disturb it."

Hastily, they pile the sand back into the hole. Much to our relief, we leave.

We continue our exploration. Soon, we come upon another burial place. The men unearth carved planks from a ship and an iron pot. We take the iron pot with us as we set out once again.

On a high hill, we find sand freshly stirred up. It smells not of Death. Men and dogs dig down once again. The men seem pleased to find baskets full of large seeds. Mercy and I sniff at them. They smell dry and dull and not at all tasty.

"Corn. We will take some with us," Bradford says. "In case the seeds we have brought with us on the *Mayflower* will not sprout in this soil. We will need something to plant in the spring."

Stephen Hopkins says, "Are we not then stealing from the savages?"

"We will find a way to pay them back another day," Bradford says. "For I have marked the place, and we will be returning."

They pour the seeds into the pot. When the pot is full, two men find a stick and push it through the handle. Balancing the stick on their shoulders, they carry the pot back toward the shore.

A raindrop hits my head. I shake it off. Soon, I am soaked by a heavy downpour. I smell snow in the droplets. The men are shivering. We stop for the night, and they build a shelter out of brush and branches. Beneath the shelter, the fire smolders and smokes and hurts our eyes.

After napping, Mercy stands guard while I sleep. Next to me, she is trembling and miserable. When I wake in the night and hear her snoring, my heart gladdens. My Furry Fellow has earned her rest.

In the morning, we shake off the dampness and continue our march through the woods. We come upon a young tree bent down to the ground. A pile of acorns lies nearby. Mercy and I growl at it. *What mischief is this?*

Stephen Hopkins bids the men examine the tree. There is a loop of rope on the end of it. "The dogs sense it. It is a native trap," he says.

Meanwhile, Bradford, bringing up the rear, unknowingly stumbles into the trap. The rope tightens around his leg. The sapling swings upward with a whipping sound. Bradford hangs upside down by one foot. His face turns dark. His eyes bug.

COLD HARBOR

Mercy barks, then stops and cocks her head when she sees that the upside-down man is smiling.

"Ho-ho! A very pretty device!" Bradford declares.

The others cut him down from the trap and take the rope with them.

"Made by the natives." Bradford dusts himself off. "And fine workmanship it is, too. As fine as any in England."

We come to the shore, where men still toil at putting together the shallop. Master Jones marvels at our prizes: the pot of corn and the rope. He laughs when they tell how Bradford stepped into the trap.

When we return to the *Mayflower,* Love, Wrestling, and Remember come running. I jump up on them and greet them. Mercy knows better than to do this. Owing to her size, she would bowl them over onto their backs.

"Did you dogs have yourselves a grand adventure?" they ask.

We wag our tails and pant.

Oh, if you only knew! Mercy whines.

"We had one of our own," says Wrestling. "You will never guess."

And then they all begin to speak at once.

"Francis made trouble. *Again,*" says Remember.

"Francis had some duck feathers," Love says.

Remember says, "Then he found an open keg of gunpowder. He filled the duck quills with powder to make a squib."

Mercy and I shiver. Squibs are things lit with fire that make a loud bang. People set them off in the streets of London Town on feast days and scare the wits out of dogs and horses alike.

"He might have left it alone at that," says Remember, "but then he spied a musket hanging on the wall."

"So he went and found himself a lit candle to ignite the musket fuse and squibs," Love says grimly.

"He climbed upon a box and took down the musket," says Wrestling. "He lit the fuse. And *BOOM! BANG! BOOM!*"

Mercy and I start, as if at a real explosion.

"It is a very good thing you were not on board," says Remember. "The noise would have hurt your poor ears. Because when the musket went off, it set off two more."

"Seamen came running from all directions," says Love. "They hauled Billington up by the collar."

"But poor Francis was as frightened as anyone," Remember says. "His eyes smarted from the smoke and his fingers were burned. He begged for forgiveness."

Standish, who has been listening to all this, says, "If the powder in that open keg had exploded, the *Mayflower* would have been nothing but driftwood rising and falling on the tide. Thanks to God for protecting this ship."

And no thanks at all to Francis Billington! says Mercy.

But when I look at him, all I see is a frightened

boy. He is older by some years than the elder Brewster lad, and yet he seems far younger to me, as if lack of love from his parents had stunted him.

The next day, while we are waiting to board the longboat, Francis approaches me. Strangely, I no longer fear him. I can see he means me no harm. He has grown timid. His fingers reach out to me. He strokes my fur.

Remember whispers, "He takes comfort from touching you, Dash. He is not such a bad sort, after all."

Francis replies, "I'm afraid of dogs. One bit me when I was still in the cradle. Do you see this scar?"

He shows her a long white mark on his arm.

"That's terrible! This dog will never bite you. Nor will Mercy," says Remember. "They are the best dogs in the world. If you are nice to them, they will be nice to you. That is true for all of us."

Francis nods slowly and goes on stroking my fur. I do not shrink from his touch. I understand that, for him, touching a dog takes courage.

"If you promise to be good," Remember tells Francis, "you can play with us today."

He scuffs his shoes against the deck. "The Brewster boys hate me."

"You might want to give them a chance. I

daresay they will give you one," says Remember.

Mercy says to me, *He is far too old to play with our lads and lass.*

No one of his own age will have him, I reply. *Perhaps friendship will improve his character.*

The shallop finally in one piece, there are thirty-four people and two dogs under sail aboard it today. John Goodman is too sick to make the trip. The cold rains have given him a chill. When we linger by his mattress, he heaves himself up and orders us to follow Master Jones. We do our master's bidding. Mercy sighs. It is difficult for her to leave John Goodman unguarded.

The shallop is but a small thing compared with the *Mayflower*. Like a child's toy, it is blown by the wind from one side of the harbor to the other. When we near the shore, the men must drag the boat across cold and mucky flats. The men are muddy and miserable. When Mercy and I get onto the beach, we shake slivers of ice from our coats.

I have never felt such cold, Mercy says.

I fear for the men, I say. *They have no fur to protect them.*

They stagger around us, sneezing and coughing and huddled into their collars. They are covered with ice from the sea spray but do not know enough to shake it off.

No sooner have we arrived onshore than the snow begins to fall.

"We will call this place Cold Harbor," says Master Jones.

"An apt-enough name," says Bradford.

By the time we make camp, the snow is deep. Mercy and I roll in it, then shake it off. I go out with Master Jones and flush some game. We bring back six ducks and four geese. That night, the men cook them in the fire pit. Our bones might be cold, but our bellies are full.

The next day, true to Bradford's word, we return to Corn Hill, the place where we dug up the seeds. The men dig up more. Then Master Jones claps his hands loudly and says we must return to the *Mayflower*. Many of the men have sickened. They sneeze and cough. We leave in such a hurry that Master Bradford does not seem to have time to leave payment for the seeds. On our way back to the harbor, we come upon yet another grave. The men dig it up, with no help from us. Mercy sits on her haunches and whimpers. I lie down with my nose resting on my paws and worry.

I do not *like the way things are going,* I say.

I agree, says Mercy.

They ought to let buried things lie, I say.

In good time, the men cry out. They have found two bundles wrapped in mats. Curiosity getting the better of me, I rise and approach as they unwrap the bundles. There is a fragrant powder within. I sneeze. In one bundle, the powder covers a collection of bones and . . . a human skull!

Ugh. I like bones as much as the next dog, but I pull back.

Bradford draws nearer. "The hair is yellow," he says. "This is no native. These are the bones of a European sailor."

In the other bundle are the bones of a small child, along with a small native Hunting Bow.

"Did the European sailor have a native child?" Bradford wonders.

The men hastily cover up the grave.

Now they are being sensible, say I.

I fear the damage is already done, says Mercy.

We move on and, later, come upon strange-looking man-made structures.

"Indian houses," Bradford says.

They are made of young trees, bent over with their ends stuck in the ground, covered with sheets of bark. Inside the houses there is room enough for a man to stand. There is a cold fire pit at the center and a smoke hole in the top. Mercy and I sniff among the clay pots and bowls and baskets and a ship's bucket.

The people here left in a hurry, I say to Mercy.

We find deer meat and some fish. We lead the humans over to show them, proud of our find. They hold their noses. The meats are ripe, but for us dogs, the riper the better. Mercy and I eat our fill.

Later, much to my distress, we make our way back to Corn Hill. The men dig up more of the seeds and load them up in bags and baskets, leaving just a few seeds behind.

Aren't you going to leave anything in payment for the natives? I ask Bradford with my eyes. But he is too cold to meet my look.

Many of the men are bent over with illness as we head back to the shore.

When we return to the *Mayflower,* the men reel off to their bunks. But Bradford hauls himself up. "What can be the matter with me?" he cries. "I forgot to leave beads in payment for the corn!"

Did I not tell you? I whine to him. *But you wouldn't listen.*

No good will come of this, says Mercy.

I heave a deep sigh. *I fear the natives will be angry with us for taking what is not ours to take.*

Mercy snorts, *I know I would be if some dog came along and dug up my bone.*

Many on the *Mayflower* are ailing with fever and chills. Death hovers. And yet, Life finds its way into the world. Another babe has been born. It is a male child and he is named Peregrine.

"What a beautiful name!" Remember says. "It is the name of a hunting bird. But it also means *traveler* or *pilgrim*."

Surely, I say to Mercy, *this creature is too small to travel.*

I hope they keep it warm, Mercy says. *This is no weather for a tender little pup.*

RAIN OF DEATH

Days later, we are back in the shallop, searching for a Safe Harbor. John Goodman is still too sick to come. Every day, it seems, Mercy and I have a new master. We sit in the bow with the pilot, a mate named Coppin. He has sailed in these parts before. He says he knows of a Safe Harbor, a place where we might settle down. We pray this is so. Everyone worries that the winter will find us without a home. The salt spray freezes on our coats. To my mind, winter has already found us. I sneeze.

As we near the shore, we see natives on the beach. They are cutting up the body of a dead whale. When they spy us, they gather arms full of whale flesh and run into the woods, whooping and hollering. We come up onto the beach. Mercy and I sniff around the whale. We would both love nothing more than to roll in it and gnaw the flesh off the bones. But the men call us away.

That day, we find more graves and empty native houses. The men collect prizes and, much to my disgust, leave not a single bead in payment. Will they never learn? That night, they build a shelter of logs with a fire pit inside. Mercy and two men stand guard at the entryway. I bed down near Mercy.

In the morning, men carry our supplies and prizes to the shallop, where it lies beached nearby.

Mercy and I follow with our eyes as the men carry their muskets to the shallop and come back empty-handed.

Is this wise? I say to Mercy.

Mercy growls, deep in her throat. *I smell natives,* she says.

I smell them, too. It is a ripe, wild, and very interesting scent and it is close by.

I spy one of them! Then more and more. They are hiding behind the trees. Our men protect themselves from the cold with clothing and boots and coats and hats. They grow fur on their faces. But the natives are naked, except for a flap of cloth around their middles, and their faces have no fur. Their hair is long in back, bound with feathers. They have Hunting Bows in their hands. I growl at them as they fit sharp sticks to the strings and lift the Hunting Bows to their cheeks.

Mercy and I bark. *Beware! We are fierce dogs and we will attack.*

One of the sticks flies from the bow with a *zing* and buries its barbed head in the log of our shelter.

Mercy and I duck our heads.

One of the men shouts, "Indians!"

The next moment, sharp sticks rain down upon us. Mercy and I flatten ourselves. Mercy is panting and growling. *Let me at them!*

"Stay, dog!" Standish says.

If you insist, Mercy huffs, and remains where she is.

The sticks land all about us. Although none pierces our flesh, these sticks smell of Death.

Beside me, Mercy yowls, *How dare they shoot sticks at our men? Just wait until I close my jaws around their necks.*

Only Standish and a few other men inside the shelter are armed with muskets. The rest of the men are unarmed. Their weapons are stowed aboard the shallop.

Through a hail of flying sticks, the unarmed men break and run for the boat.

From the beach, one of them shouts out to Standish, "We are safe at the boat! We have our muskets, but no fire to light the fuses! Our weapons are useless!"

Standish fires his gun at the natives. Their sticks

fly far more thickly than his shot. But neither shot nor sticks seem to find their mark in flesh.

"Be of stout heart!" Standish calls out to the men trapped at the boat.

Then another man from the shelter bends to the fire and lifts a burning log in his arms. He runs with it toward the beach. Death Sticks pursue him, but they do not find him.

In no time, there are muskets firing from both the shelter and the boat.

Soon, we hear the natives cry out, "Woach! Woach! Ha! Ha! Hach! Woach!"

The flurry of Death Sticks dies back, then ceases. Mercy and I leap to our feet and run, barking, toward the woods. But the natives have vanished.

After them! says Mercy.

I am all for it, but Standish whistles and claps his hands. "Get back here, you dogs!" he shouts.

Mercy continues to run. I call her back with my most shrill bark.

She stops and turns to look at me.

Our place is with the men, I remind her. *They may still be in danger.*

Reluctantly, Mercy follows me back to the camp.

As rain starts to fall, I help the men gather the fallen sticks, offering them up in my mouth.

"Good boy," Bradford says to me. "You fetch arrows as well as you do fowl."

Arrows, the men call these Death Sticks. Mercy sniffs at them and snarls. She attacks one of them. She shakes it and will not rest until it falls from her mouth in splinters. The men laugh.

I sniff at the arrows with interest. At one end, they are feathered, like birds' wings. At the other is a barb made of stone or deer antler or brass.

We go to the shallop. The wind has picked up, and the rain has turned to sleet. The men push the shallop into the water. We will leave this place. I sneeze with relief and shake my head.

There is no Safe Harbor for us here.

The wind blows harder. The men hunch into their collars, miserable and shivering, their face fur coated with ice. I shelter in the lee of my big,

warm Mercy. I hear the great hound panting and whining.

"Be of good cheer!" Mate Coppin cries out above the wind. "I know our Safe Harbor is just ahead."

The current is so powerful, it wrenches the steering board from its place in the stern. We lose the wind, and the sails fall limp. Two men take up oars and row the boat until we catch the wind again. We are running smoothly before it when, all of a sudden, the mast splinters! A wet sail collapses on top of us. The men work the oars and move us toward shore with the last of their strength.

But the shore looks far from safe. The sleet is thickening to snow. Before us, the waves rise up and smash themselves upon the rocks. Mate Coppin says, "This place is unfamiliar to me."

All is lost.

What will become of us? Mercy whimpers.

Finally, rounding a point, the boat meets up with gentler waters surrounding a small island. The seas that lie before us are shallow and calm.

The men drag the shallop onto the beach and build a fire. We spend our time resting, drying our coats, warming our bones, and finding a straight tree to make a new mast.

The next morning is the Praying Day. The sun shines, yet the winds blow bitter cold. While the men pray, Mercy and I nose around. I find the crushed body of a seagull to roll in. Mercy finds a rodent. We sleep, curled up together in the sand.

The following day, we cross from the island to the mainland and march up a high hill. A brook of sweet water babbles. Nearby, there are cornfields gone fallow from lack of use but no sign of native houses.

Looking around, Bradford says, "This is the harbor Captain John Smith mapped on his voyage here in 1613: fresh water, planting fields, and a hill with a clear view of the coast. It is called New Plymouth, and it is a good thing we have found it, for now, surely, the Heart of Winter is upon us."

Lions in the Night!

The hill where we will build our new home is high, but flat on top. It overlooks a salty marsh teeming with birds and a long stretch of coastline. While the colonists walk about, planning where the houses and other buildings will sit, Mercy and I follow our noses. We find human bones, some jutting up out of the earth. Skulls lie in plain sight, unburied. The bones are bleached white, and yet our noses tell us: the people here died of some dread disease.

Perhaps that is why this place is so sad and empty and shunned.

Mercy and I remain onshore with a small party. The rest return to the *Mayflower.* The ship has followed us to this harbor and lies anchored offshore, close enough for us to see its lights twinkling at night. Tomorrow, more men will come ashore and start the building. But in the night, such a storm comes up as to nearly blow us all away. Mercy howls almost as loudly as the wind.

The gale continues to rage all through the following day. No building can be done. I rouse myself to go hunting with John Goodman, who is sickly but able to lift his musket.

The fire is barely hot enough to cook the fowl, and the men tear at it with their teeth. The meat is practically raw. They complain bitterly. There are bloody scraps aplenty for the big girl and me to feast upon. That night, we stare out to sea and watch the *Mayflower* buck the waves. It takes two anchors to hold her down.

Finally, the clouds flee before the wind and uncover a sun as pale as a winter egg yolk. Men come ashore. Their faces are long.

"We have lost three more to sickness," one of them reports.

Later, more of the healthy ones leave the ship, including the lads and lass. The children run about, heedless of the cold. Francis Billington belongs to the pack now. We lead the children to our favorite places and show them the bones.

Francis rears back. "The Evil Eye watches this place!"

"Don't even *say* that," Remember says, clutching herself and gazing around uneasily.

Wrestling, however, seems to warm to this notion. Like Pirates, the Evil Eye will make a good game.

"Pishposh," says Love. "God smiles upon this place. Our father says so."

One of the colonists spies us in a huddle. "This is no time for idle play," he says. "If you are healthy, you will work."

We lose our playmates. All around us, there is a great hustle and bustle. The men cut down trees with axes.

"Watch out below!" they cry as the trees topple with an earth-shaking thud.

Teams of men rope the timber and haul it up the hill.

Mercy and I must scramble to stay out from underfoot.

Francis says, "It is Christmastime. Back home in London, they'll be resting and feasting, but here it is nothing but work, from sunup to sundown."

Night falls. The forests around us rise up, dark and cold. From their depths, we can hear the chanting of the natives. We smell the smoke from their fires. The colonists grow uneasy. They swap their axes for muskets. Many return to the *Mayflower*, leaving a few brave souls—and us dogs—behind.

With daylight, workers return from the ship. They set to building the first house on the hillside. It is big and takes many days to raise. The walls of the house are split pieces of wood over a frame of heavy, squared oak posts and beams. The men cover it with a muddy mixture called daub. The roof is made of reeds and cattails from the marsh below. Smoke from the fire goes out a hole in the roof. Now we have a place to shelter when the others return nightly to the *Mayflower*. It is called the Common House.

Next, the men lay boards across the top of the hill. But no walls go up. The platform remains there, empty and awaiting some use that is mysterious to Mercy and me. We will use it in the meantime for our own purposes. I lift my leg, and Mercy squats at its corners. The men laugh.

The colonists lay out one street that runs from the platform down to the sea, and another that crosses it, leading to the brook. Along both sides of the street they start to build more houses, one for each family. Men without mates will stay with families. John Goodman has no mate. Happily for us, he—and we—will stay with the Brewsters. Will there be room for everyone and Mercy, too? Mercy huddles down and tries to make herself smaller than she is, which is no mean feat for such a big dog. Then a man whistles for her. Poor Mercy. It is a good thing she sneaks naps during the day. Her nights must ever be given over to guard duty.

One day, while Bradford hammers a peg, he drops his mallet and falls to the ground. I run to his side and lick his face. It is cold and salty. They carry him off to the Common House. In the days that follow, it becomes the Sick House as more colonists fall ill. There is scarcely room inside for all who ail. William Brewster and Standish, among the few healthy ones, are left to tend the fires and feed and wash the sick. Mercy and I whine with worry. All building comes to a halt.

Meanwhile, on board the *Mayflower*, the seamen have also fallen sick. Mercy frets that they will all die and leave us to run wild. I worry, too, but I do not let on to my Furry Fellow.

There could be worse things, I point out to Mercy. *We could fall ill, along with the rest.* But happily, we dogs remain hale and hearty.

On another day, we go with John Goodman and Peter Browne into the marsh to cut thatch for the roofs of the new houses. All morning, we listen to the whistle of their sickles as they slice through the reeds. The men pile the reeds in batches and tie them in bundles. When the sun is high, the men lean against a tree and eat hard bread and cheese. Mercy and I lie nearby with our heads resting on our paws and watch for falling crumbs. Our jaws snap as we catch each delicious morsel.

The meal over, John Goodman says, "You dogs have gotten precious little exercise lately. Let us take you for a walk."

We amble off into the woods. Mercy and I sniff high and low. Mercy's head lifts. Her nostrils twitch in the wind.

Deer! she says to me. And off we go! I do my best to keep up, but her legs are so much longer than mine. We chase the deer until we lose the line of scent. When our master and Peter Browne catch up with us, they are panting and covered in brambles.

"You two led us on a merry chase," our master says, bending over to catch his breath.

Peter Browne's brow wrinkles. "The sun has gone behind the clouds," he says. "I have not the slightest clue where we are."

We dogs sniff around. The wind has shifted, and we have lost the scent of our path. The men follow us. But we pull up short, baffled. Then we hear the patter of rain on the bare branches. The rain soon whitens to snow. Darkness falls.

We come upon a native house. It is empty inside, its fire pit cold. The men have no flint, so we cannot have a firc. They sleep on the ground. "Like dogs," they say bitterly.

In the night, we all awake at once to shrill cries. Mercy leaps up and runs to the door.

What is that noise? I ask.

Mercy says, *Wild and vicious beasts. Let's go out there and get them.*

But John Goodman claps a hand on her collar. "Lions," he says. "They'll tear you to pieces, Mercy. Stay put, big girl."

If only I could sink my teeth into them, Mercy says. With great difficulty, she settles down by my side. But I can feel her twitching. Every time her head nods, the lions let out another cry. It is as if they are taunting her.

"If the lions come," John Goodman says to Peter, "we will climb a tree. I pray that lions cannot climb trees. We will leave Mercy to fight them."

Did you hear that? Mercy says. *They know I will protect them from the lions.*

I do not know what a lion is, but I like not the smell. It reeks of my least favorite creature: cat!

Worry not, my little friend, says Mercy. *I will defend you, too. Remember that, in my time, I have fought bears. How much more ferocious can lions be?*

Possibly very ferocious, I think uneasily. Size gives Mercy a confidence I do not have. Some small dogs believe themselves to be big. I have no such belief.

After a while, the men are too nervous to sleep. Instead, they stand outside, holding their sickles like weapons.

The rising sun silences the lions. We strike out again in search of Plymouth. It is cold and the snow is deep. The teeth of winter have bitten so hard into John Goodman's feet that he is limping by the time we arrive home.

THE WELCOMING PARTY

Some days later, John Goodman's feet are still too sore for duck hunting. I offer to lick them, but he waves me off.

"Go with Peter and help him hunt some fowl," he says weakly.

With a reluctant sigh, I leave with Peter Browne for the marsh. I am zigzagging through the cattails when I smell something that is not fowl.

Moments pass, and I see a line of natives walking through the marsh in the direction of our home. How silently they move!

I dash back to Peter Browne, where he nestles on his belly in the reeds. He is surprised to see me. And none too happy.

"Get back there and find some ducks!" he says.

I point my nose toward the natives. Peter Browne sees them now, too: the long line of tall, naked men making for Plymouth.

"We must warn the others!" he whispers.

He leaps to his feet. As silently as we can, we run ahead of the natives all the way to the village. The colonists who are healthy are busy building their houses. Peter sounds the alarm, clanging the ship's bell that now hangs outside the Common House. The men drop their mallets and saws and run to arm themselves with muskets and swords.

Everyone stands in quiet readiness. Mercy and

I pant and watch the forest. We are ready, too.

But the natives never come.

That night, we dogs spy the light of a great fire burning in the marsh not so far from where Peter Browne and I had been hunting. Even from here, I can smell the duck fat hitting the fire.

I know as surely as my stomach gurgles that they got the ducks I might have flushed.

In the days that follow, I feel the eyes of the natives on us. Mercy and I are nervous and short of temper. The children know not to bother us lest we curl our lips and growl at them. Meanwhile, Death hovers, claiming at least one colonist a day over the long winter months. Whole families are now gone. The men take Mercy and me up the hill behind the houses under cover of darkness. They go to bury the bodies of the dead. It is their belief that the natives will not see what they are up to.

"The savages must not find out," Standish says.

But as Mercy and I know all too well, the natives see everything. Not only do we feel their eyes upon us. We smell them moving ever closer. We hear faint rustlings in the undergrowth.

We make many such trips into the night to dig shallow graves. By the time spring arrives, our numbers are cut in half.

When they first play the game, we dogs do not understand. Standish rings the bell. The sick are dragged from the Common House and propped up with muskets in hand. Mercy and I are baffled. We have not picked up the scent of natives. Why the excitement? When everyone is outside and armed, Standish tells them to go back to their business. The sick are dragged back to their mattresses. The building resumes. Until the next time they ring the bell to play the game.

"I know it must be very confusing for you dogs," Remember says to us. "But we are practicing in the event of a real Indian raid."

Practicing for a raid? I say to Mercy. *People are so odd.*

Perhaps we should practice, too, Mercy suggests.

And so, whenever the bell rings, Mercy and I join the men with muskets, our fur bristling and our teeth bared. Mercy sometimes forgets it is a game and I have to bark at her by way of reminder.

I am a silly dog, aren't I? she says.

The colonists are meeting one day outside the Common House. Mercy and I lie at John Goodman's feet. Suddenly, Mercy and I lift our noses.

Our bodies stiffen. Our noses point in the same direction. *Natives!* we say with a low growl.

John Goodman whispers, "What is it, dogs? What do you smell?"

Then he sees. On the hill across the brook two natives stand. John Goodman nudges the man next to him. The elbows make their way up and down the rows of men. Soon, in tense silence, colonists and natives are staring at each other across the small valley that separates them.

At the word from Standish, the men run to fetch their weapons. They return to find that the natives have not moved. Mercy and I take our places by the colonists' sides. The natives raise their arms and sweep them through the air in a sign that I, as a dog, know to mean, *Come here!*

Standish says, *No, you come here!* with a sign of his own. The natives remain rooted. Finally, Standish and Stephen Hopkins make the first move.

We watch as they trudge down our hill. Before crossing the brook, Standish lays down his musket. Hopkins has no weapon. With arms raised above their heads, they climb up the hill to meet the natives.

When a dog rolls over and shows its belly to another dog, it is to say, *See? I will not hurt you. And I trust that you will not hurt me, even though I am offering you ample opportunity to do so.* The men's raised arms are just such a signal.

But before the men have reached the top of the hill, the natives have turned and run down the other side, giving out with a shrill cry. Beyond the hill, we hear the answering cry of many, many more natives.

That afternoon, the colonists make several trips to the anchored *Mayflower*. Each time they return, the shallop rides low in the water. The shallop carries cannons.

Mercy and I watch fretfully as the men haul the heavy cannons up the hill. They sweat and strain and snarl at each other. We dogs stand clear, for we fear these big guns. We have heard their ferocious roar back in England. We have seen them spew fire. The noise sets our teeth on edge and our ears to ringing.

Finally, we know what the flat wooden platform at the top of our hill is for. The colonists set up the cannons there and aim their gaping mouths at the hill where the natives stood.

As I sit staring uneasily at the great guns, Master Jones says, "Come with me, Dash, and make yourself useful."

I follow the brave man down into the marsh, where I lose myself in my work. Quickly, I flush a goose, a crane, and a mallard, and then still more fowl. Master Jones and I work well together. That night, thanks to the two of us, we enjoy a small feast. The colonists seem at peace now that the cannons keep watch for them.

We dogs sit by the fire, Wrestling and Love and Remember wrapping their arms around us. After a bit, they make room for Francis Billington. He works an arm around my neck and strokes my ear. *Is this the same boy,* I wonder, *who used to toss his moldy boot at me?*

In the days that follow, I smell the green of spring and hear a racket of new birds in the trees. One late afternoon, on the warmest day yet, I spy a lone native standing atop that same hill across the brook from us. John Goodman sees him, too. He runs to sound the alarm.

The men reach for their muskets. The native sets off down the hill in our direction. The colonists ready their muskets, but the native shows no fear as he marches up the brook road and walks past the drawn guns. Mercy and I run to protect the children and their mothers. The native is making straight for us. Yet no one stops him. The colonists are like meek rabbits, frozen before the wolf.

Strangely, neither does Mercy make any move to attack or even to growl.

Maybe I am silly, but I trust him, she says thoughtfully. *He smells good.*

He is certainly tall, say I. He is taller than the colonists, straight and noble. I wag my tail and look up into his dark eyes. He meets my gaze with kindness, reaches a hand down, and shows me his palm. I sniff at it. The smell is good. I lick his palm, and he pats my head.

Mercy is right. This is just a man, like all other men. And he means us no harm. He walks on.

One of the colonists finally takes courage. He holds up a hand that says to the native, *Stop right here.*

The native stops. He smiles. He raises his hand and touches the side of his head in what seems to be an English soldier's salute.

"Welcome, Englishmen!" says he.

SAMOSET

Like the natives I have seen in the woods, this one is almost naked, except for the flaps of cloth at his waist. He seems not to feel the cold. He carries a bow and two arrows: one sharp-tipped, the other with no tip at all. *He will not release these arrows from his bow,* I think. The arrows carry a message. They say, *We will either fight or be friends.*

"I am surprised the poor soul doesn't catch his death. There's nary a stitch on him," one of the women mutters to another, shaking her head.

John Goodman takes his coat and drapes it gently over the Indian's broad shoulders.

Bradford says, "We have water and food."

The native nods eagerly.

Stephen Hopkins's house is nearby. Hopkins bids him enter, and Elizabeth Hopkins fills a plate for him: a biscuit and cheese and a slice of duck meat. As many of us as can fit crowd inside the Hopkins house. My mouth waters at the smell of the food.

The native sits on the floor and eats while we watch. Mercy and I hunker down, edging ever closer to him. The lads and lass follow along behind us. They sit and stroke our coats as they listen and watch. The native smacks his lips when he bites into the duck meat.

I sit up a little taller and wag my tail. *I flushed*

that duck myself and brought it to my master without a single tooth mark on it, I say with an eager yip. *I will do the same for you. You have but to ask me.*

The native looks up and seems to understand me. He reaches out and pats my head. Then he looks to the colonists. "I am Samoset," he says.

The colonists mutter. The bravest among them, including Bradford, name themselves, one after the other. Slowly, the native repeats their names.

I am Dash, I say eagerly when my turn comes. *And this big girl here is Mercy. We are at your service.*

Samoset reaches out and claps a hand over Mercy's head. He says, "I am not from this place. I am from up north in Monhegan, where English fishers come to shore. They teach me to speak your tongue."

The colonists listen in awed silence.

Mercy and I watch the food make the trip from the bowl to his mouth, never once breaking our gaze. He stops, feeling our eyes on him. He tosses us some bits, which we catch and eat. Mercy licks her chops and waits for more. She is already in love with him—I can tell by the look in her big, moist eyes. I must confess to my own fascination.

"All the people once living here have died of English Plague," says the native.

"That explains the bones," whispers Love.

"What did I tell you?" Francis says. "The Evil Eye watches this place."

"Shhh," says Love.

"The nearest people are the Pokanoket Wampanoag, who live southwest of here. Massasoit is their sachem."

"Pssst." Wrestling elbows Love. "What is a *sachem?*"

"A *sachem,*" says Samoset, eyeing Wrestling, "is a *leader. A wise one.* It is the Nauset Wampanoag whose corn you stole. Nauset warriors attacked you in your camp. We see all. We watch all."

The colonists shift awkwardly on their feet. They hang their heads, like dogs who know when they have done wrong.

Bradford clears his throat. "Tell the Nauset that we will gladly repay them for the corn," he says.

The native smiles. "The Nauset already hate the English. Once, the English stole twenty Nauset men and never brought them back."

Love frowns. "We would never be so cruel."

"You have no idea how cruel some Englishmen can be," Francis says.

This native must have the ears of a terrier, for his eyes find Francis. He smiles. Francis returns a brave smile.

"My English is not so good. But I know one who speaks very good English. Tisquantum, a man without people, separated from his tribe. I will bring him to you. Then we will talk. Eat duck. Drink beer."

When Samoset finishes his meal, he hands his bowl to Mistress Hopkins. He folds his arms across his chest and lies down. "I will sleep here."

The colonists stare at him in wonder.

Reluctantly, we leave the house and let the native sleep.

In the morning when we wake, the native is gone.

Mercy, awake before I was, saw him leave. She tells me, *He left with gifts: a knife, a ring, and a bracelet. Do you think he will return?*

I hope so, I say.

Some days later, Samoset returns to us with Tisquantum—whom the colonists will come to call Squanto—and three other Wampanoag men. Mercy and I meet them as they cross the brook. We walk them up the hill. They carry gifts of furs and dried fish to trade. Once again, they go to the Hopkins house and eat and drink while as many as can fit into the house watch.

"I have seen the world," says Squanto. He

speaks like an Englishman boasting in a pub. "I have been to Spain and to England. If Massasoit is as wise a sachem as I think he is, the Wampanoag will make allies of the English to protect them from their Narragansett neighbors."

Not long after the meal, new natives appear on the hill. One of them is a big, strong man, his face painted and his body shining with grease. "That is Massasoit," says Squanto.

Squanto goes over to the hill and returns. "Massasoit would like to speak to one of you. But he wants one of the colonists as a hostage to ensure his own safety."

Edward Winslow volunteers, bearing gifts for the sachem. But first he dons a soldier's armor and arms. I watch him approach the sachem. He gives him biscuits and drink. Winslow remains behind while Massasoit and twenty Wampanoag cross back over to us. The colonists watch and worry.

The father of Love and Wrestling has prepared a meeting place. In front of one of the partially built houses, he has laid down a carpet with cushions. In full soldiers' armor and armed with swords, the menfolk march to the house, trumpets blaring and drums rolling. It is a small parade, the first in this new land.

Carver, the man who has been named "Governor of Plymouth," approaches Massasoit. He bows and kisses his hand. The sachem kisses Carver's hand. They sit on the pillows, share a drink, and talk.

I wriggle to the front of the crowd. Massasoit is a big man, far bigger than any colonist. He has many soldiers, far more than the armed men among the colonists, and all taller by far than Captain Standish. And yet he trembles. Perhaps Squanto is

right. Massasoit needs the colonists to protect him from his Narragansett neighbors. This meeting is an important one for him.

After the meeting, everyone is happy. They have drawn up another compact, this one between the English and the Wampanoag. Bradford explains the agreement to the lads and lass. The English and Wampanoag promise not to hurt each other, but to hurt those who would hurt either of them. If they borrow each other's tools, they will return them. They will not carry weapons to their meetings.

In short, each group has rolled over and shown its belly to the other.

Hills Made of Fish

We sit on the shore with the colonists as they watch the good ship *Mayflower* sail away, bound for England, laden with the pelts of beaver and sweet-smelling sassafras.

When the ship has disappeared from sight, Mercy and I look to Squanto and ask with our eyes, *What next?*

And Squanto knows!

He leads us all to the babbling brook. "Catch as

many fish as you can," he tells the colonists. "The fish will make your plants grow."

Mercy runs up and down the bank, as if trying to herd the fish. But the fish pay her no heed. She is no herder.

The colonists have better luck. With baskets, they catch the running fish and haul them flapping from the brook.

Mercy barks and leaps about. The flashing fish excite her. Silly dog!

Carrying the heavy baskets of dripping fish, the colonists follow Squanto up to the fields. The men take up long sticks with rocks lashed to the ends. Squanto shows them how to stir up the dirt, then bury the fish in the mounds with the corn seeds.

Oh, joy! A new game! says Mercy. Her digging paws a blur, she burrows down into one of the mounds and comes up with a fish in her mouth.

William Brewster scolds her. Ears flattened, Mercy drops the filthy fish at his feet. *I'm sorry!*

Brewster reburies the fish, laughing softly to himself.

The colonists work all day, until the field is filled with mounds. Mercy gazes upon them and sighs. *Oh, the fun I could have had!*

In the days and weeks that follow, the rains fall

and the sun shines. Mercy and I chase each other between the hillocks. Soon, little shoots poke out from the top of each mound.

"The corn has sprouted!" Squanto cries joyfully. "Time to plant the beans and squash."

They plant the seeds at the base of each new corn shoot. Before long, these seeds sprout and twist up the cornstalks.

One morning, a strange dog wanders into the colony. He has a coat the color of wheat and is about my size. After we greet each other, circling and sniffing with tails high, Mercy falls to her haunches, hind end in the air, tail wagging eagerly. *There are too few dogs in this place for us to make enemies of you,* she says. *Let's play.*

I thought I smelled a female, says the stranger. *You're a big one, too!*

The fur on my back rises. *She's my* big friend,

I snarl. *Not yours. Stay away from her, I tell you!*

The strange dog rolls onto his back and shows me his belly. *I didn't mean any harm. Can't we just be friends?*

I start to growl, but Mercy nuzzles me. *Dash. Be good.*

I settle down, and I shake off my anger. *I am called Dash, and this is Mercy.*

I am Wompey, he says. *I am a village dog and I do as I am told, but when I smell a female, I cannot help myself. I go after her, no matter how far away she may be.*

Are there more big dogs like you where you come from? Wompey asks Mercy.

Some, she says.

We have dogs of all shapes and sizes in England, I tell him. *Most of us are working dogs. Some dogs herd sheep, and others dig tunnels and catch rats. Still others fish and hunt. People call the different dogs breeds. Some of us are a mixture of breeds. People call them mongrels.*

Here we have no breeds, says Wompey. *We guard our masters.*

You had best return to your master now before he misses you, I advise.

Perhaps we will see you again, says Mercy.

Perhaps, says Wompey.

After Wompey goes, Mercy says to me, *Dash, I do believe you are jealous.*

I am nothing of the kind, say I, and quickly search for a flea to scratch.

In these warm, long days the children continue to help with tasks, but there is more time for play. We dogs follow to make sure they stay out of harm's way. They quickly learn where the good swimming holes are. One hot and windless day, they even brave a swim in the ocean. Mercy sits at the edge of the water and whimpers as their sleek heads bob. She leaps up and barks whenever their heads disappear.

On another day, Love and Wrestling and Francis cut branches from trees and attempt to make bows and arrows. They lift the crude bows to their cheeks and release the arrows, aiming at rabbits and squirrels. I retrieve the arrows and bring them to the children. Their bows are not so strong, nor their aim so true, that small animals are in any real danger. Mercy and I pose a much greater danger.

Later in the summer, Bradford orders Winslow and Hopkins to go to Pokanoket, the home of Massasoit. Bradford was named the new governor after Carver fell ill and died.

"They know the way to *our* settlement. We

must learn the way to theirs," Bradford says.

We dogs go with them. They bear gifts for Massasoit and food for the trail. We set out with Squanto.

On the second day, we meet up with a group of natives returning from the seashore. They are laden with sacks packed with seaweed and armored sea creatures that snap.

Mercy barks and dances around them.

Stay away from Dash! she says. *I warn you!*

The natives laugh. They say to Squanto, "Your big dog is not fond of lobsters."

The big dog remembers how, not so long ago, I came upon one of these clawed creatures in the shallows of the harbor. I sniffed it and—*snap!*—it closed its fierce claws around my snout. I yelped and swung my head, finally flinging the creature loose. But my nose! It throbbed for days afterward.

I will not tangle with them anytime soon.

As the sun sets, we come upon natives fishing
in the river. We camp in the nearby fields, and they
share their fish with our men. Mercy and I wander
off and chase down a rabbit and a family of field

mice. The next day, some of these natives stay with our group, following us along the riverbank.

We stop at midday. Squanto says, "Here, we must cross the river, where it is shallow."

The men remove their breeches. Holding their muskets and bedrolls and clothing above their heads, they wade across the river. Mercy and I paddle alongside them, our heads high.

Suddenly, on the far bank, two natives rise up out of the reeds. Their bows are drawn and loaded with arrows. Mercy and I don't know whether to attack or turn around and swim back to shore. We swim in small, frantic circles while we wait for the men to decide.

The natives who have joined us cry out and wave their hands. The armed ones hear familiar voices and lower their bows. It is good to have friends among the natives.

When we arrive in the Wampanoag village of Pokanoket, Massasoit is nowhere to be found. We must wait for him to return from a hunting trip. When he finally arrives, Hopkins and Winslow fire their guns in the air to greet him.

Why must they fire their guns needlessly? Mercy asks me, rubbing an ear with a paw.

As a hunting dog, I am used to the sound of guns.

Sometimes they shoot when they are happy, I say. *Have I not said that humans are odd?*

Hopkins and Winslow present the sachem with gifts they have brought: a heavy copper chain and a fine English coat. Massasoit dons them and struts about. He speaks to his people in a proud and boastful voice.

The natives chant.

We watch the faces of Hopkins and Winslow.

They are weary from the trail. We hear the loud growling of their stomachs. They have fired their muskets to honor Massasoit. They have given him gifts. When will Massasoit honor his guests with food?

Darkness falls, and still no food. The sachem offers the visitors a place to sleep in his own house. Mercy and I slip off and catch some dinner for ourselves. We return to discover the two colonists wide awake in a cloud of fleas.

Mercy and I already have sufficient fleas. We sleep outside the house. But I am awakened in the night by my Furry Friend as she snaps in vain at thick swarms of buzzing insects.

The next day, sachems from nearby villages come to see the visitors from Plymouth. They run races. They play a game with stones and sticks. They beat drums and play flutes. The colonists fire their guns. Mercy suffers the racket in silence. Massasoit serves up two fish. They are large fish, but there are many mouths to feed. Winslow and Hopkins make do with but a few bites.

On the third day, the colonists leave the village. Squanto stays behind. He will go to other villages and trade trinkets and beads in exchange for furs.

The first thing the men have me do is retrieve some fowl so they can fill their empty stomachs. Then we help them retrace our steps back to Plymouth. When we arrive, Love, Wrestling, Remember, and Francis run down the hill to greet us.

It is Francis who speaks first, his chest heaving and his face drawn and pale. "My brother, John, is missing!" he says.

"He is up to some mischief," says Wrestling.

"Or he wandered off somewhere and got lost," Remember says.

"Or eaten by a wild animal," adds Love.

"He has never been a very good brother to me," Francis says. "Still, I would not have him eaten by some wild animal."

Mercy's lip curls. *Show me this wild animal,* she says. *I will tear it apart with my teeth.*

In the days that follow, Mercy and I help search the woods for John Billington. But we catch not even the faintest whiff of the lad.

A native arrives. He carries word from Pokanoket: John Billington has been found and is staying with the Nauset Wampanoag!

Nauset? My ears perk up. Nauset are the natives whose corn the colonists stole. This does not bode well.

There is no love lost here for John Billington, but the colonists know they must find him and bring him back to Plymouth.

Standish and a band of men depart in the shallop. Weapons in hand, they are off to get John Billington. There is no room in the shallop for dogs. We whine. We want to go along and help, but we are told to stay, so stay we do. While the men are gone, we do what we can to comfort the children, Francis especially.

A few days later, the men come back with John. Francis runs up to him and gives him a bashful hug. The rest of us approach the boy shyly. He smells of the Nauset, but he looks well enough. Rather than frightened, he seems proud.

"They traded me in exchange for an English knife," he tells us. "And look what the Nauset gave me. I am one of them now." John Billington wears a necklace of beads. "I was never in any danger. I was their guest of honor."

But Standish tells us a different story: "The

Nauset found him wandering lost in the woods, living on roots and nuts. They took him. Their thinking was: they stole our corn, now we will steal their boy."

Standish goes on, "We found him near the place where we had taken the corn. Corn Hill now teems with Indians. To think that we landed in the middle of their territory and never knew it. I told them that we would pay them for the corn. They are satisfied. But now we have *another* problem. Just as we were leaving, they said that yet a third tribe, the Narragansett, have gone to war with the Wampanoag. They have captured Massasoit."

Bradford's face is grim. "According to our treaty, Massasoit's enemy is ours. That means we are now at war with the Narragansett."

10

WAR AND PEACE

The men make ready for war. The children do their chores, fetching water and gathering firewood. They speak in low, fearful voices. One morning, just as the men are preparing to leave, who should appear but Massasoit! The Narragansett have set him down, unharmed, in the woods near the settlement.

I don't understand. Does this mean we are not at war after all? Mercy wonders.

I, too, am confused. *Perhaps it is all a game.*

But it is no game. The lads and lass squat in a circle and speak in worried voices.

Love says, "We may go to war yet. My father says that we colonists are the cause of the war between the Wampanoag and the Narragansett. A Wampanoag warrior and sachem named Corbitant has aligned himself with the Narragansett. He does not like the compact between the Pokanoket and the colonists. Corbitant wants to break it. He is traveling around to all the native villages, urging them to rise up against Massasoit."

Bradford asks Squanto to spy on this Corbitant fellow.

"We must be ready to go to war at a moment's notice," says Wrestling, holding his bow to his chest. "What say you dogs? Are you ready?"

Mercy pulls herself up to her full height. *I am ready*, she says.

Not I. I am a bird dog, not a war dog.

Even with war in the air, life must go on. As the colonists wait for the return of Squanto, they begin to bring in the harvest. They have corn, beans, squash, and some English crops—wheat, barley and peas—even though these did not grow as well.

One day, a native runs into the settlement. His chest heaves. He has run all the way from Pokanoket with the news. We dogs sniff at his feet. He smells of all the places he has run. He smells of bravery, too! *What news?* we dogs wonder as we stare up at him eagerly.

"Squanto is taken by Corbitant and feared dead!" the native reports.

Bradford's face is hard. He says, "If they kill

him, we will take our revenge. We must show them that those who kill our friends are our enemies."

I remain behind while Mercy goes with the men who follow the messenger to Corbitant's village. For the many days she is gone, I mope about. Life without Mercy is without joy.

When Mercy returns after a few days, I am so happy that I run to her and dance on my hind legs.

But her ears and tail droop. She is bone weary and covered with mud, as are the men with her. Among them are two native strangers, a man and a woman.

Mercy tells me, *Oh, the time I have had! When we got to the home of Corbitant, there were some men, and many women and children. But Corbitant was nowhere in sight. One young man climbed through the smoke hole and hollered for him to show his face. Women and children wept and begged for their lives. In the confusion, muskets went off. Two natives were hurt. We have brought them home with us to bind their wounds.*

"Does Squanto still live?" Bradford asks.

"Aye," says Standish. "But Corbitant and his men fled before we got there. The raid was a failure."

For the next few days, the men and women of Plymouth walk around in grim silence.

I don't like this at all, Mercy says.

We still do not know what has become of Squanto, say I. Without Squanto, the colonists would be helpless. Only he can teach us how to live here.

That very afternoon, Squanto walks into our village. The colonists cry out with joy and gather round to greet him. We dogs lick his hands.

"I have good news. The word is that the English attack on Corbitant's village was powerful and fierce," he reports to Bradford.

Could this be so when our own men had returned home with tails drooping?

"Whether or not you believe you won, you have struck fear in the hearts of the Narragansett who went against Massasoit," Squanto says.

Not long after this, nine sachems, including Corbitant, arrive at Plymouth. Mercy and I make bold and trot up to them. We sniff at their empty hands. They meet with Bradford in the Common House. They pass a pipe around in a circle. Mercy sniffs it and sneezes. The smell is unpleasant to us dogs but not so to the natives and colonists. For them, it is the smell of peace. We leave the house in search of more pleasing scents.

"The worst is over," Love says later to Wrestling and Francis and Remember. "My father says the sachems have sworn to be loyal to King James. The Nauset have forgiven us for taking their corn. And we have made peace with the natives. All is well now, or so the grown-ups believe."

Everyone works together to bring in the rest of the harvest. There are baskets overflowing with corn and squash and beans. The marshes and fields teem with more birds than I have ever seen. I go forth with Peter Browne and flush them from the undergrowth. I bring back so many that, at each day's end, my jaws are sore. At night I dream of chasing birds. My legs twitch and my jaws snap.

William Bradford calls the colonists together. He tells them it is time for a huge feast. "Now that we have gathered the fruits of our labors, it is time we rejoice together . . . in a more special manner."

The feast day arrives. Then Massasoit arrives with more than ninety Wampanoag men! They bear the carcasses of slain deer. Excitement rings in the air.

Colonists and natives build many cook fires.
Mercy and I, along with our friend Wompey, run
from fire to fire, where deer and game fowl turn on
spits. Pots of fish and turkey meat bubble. There
are ears of corn, fish, lobsters, and clams smolder-
ing in pits, layered in seaweed. Mercy licks her
chops. The very air tastes good enough to eat.

When the food is cooked, some of the

colonists and natives squat or recline around the fires. Others sit at tables made from planks resting across barrels. We dogs stake our places near the youngest children, where the most food drops between hand and mouth.

After the meal, there are footraces and games of Hub-Hub. The children play with dolls made of cloth and corn husks. Here and there, natives sing and colonists listen and nod with pleasure. As the sun sets, I nestle down next to Mercy. I yawn widely and lower my head onto my paws.

No sooner am I settled in than the lads and lass come and throw themselves down beside us. Mercy lifts her sleepy head. Seeing that she is surrounded by friends, she drops her head back onto her paws. I sigh deeply.

My belly is as full as my heart. In this land where once we faced starvation and cold and lived in fear of the natives, I am grateful that there is now a bounty of food to eat and fellowship to enjoy.

Just as I am drifting off, Mercy opens one eye and says to me, *I have a belly full of pups, Dash.*

I lift my head. I thought she had a new smell. *Mine?* I ask.

Well, of course, yours. Who is being a silly dog now?

Me? A father? My mind races ahead. What will our pups look like? Will they be big and strong? Or small and quick? Guard dogs or bird dogs? Or a cunning mixture of the two? Like everything else in our new land, this promises to be a grand adventure.

And I, for one, cannot wait!

APPENDIX

More About the English Springer Spaniel

Springer Spaniels in History

As early as seventeen years after the birth of Christ, spaniels were mentioned in the Irish laws as having been given as gifts to the king. The word *spaniel* is thought to come from either the Roman word for *Spain, Hispania,* or the French phrase *chiens de l'Espagnol,* which means *dogs of the Spanish.* The breed was probably brought north from Spain by Roman armies as early as 200 BC, when they ventured forth to conquer what is now France and Great Britain.

In 1387, Gaston Phébus, a warrior and hunter, describes spaniels in his book, *Livre de la chasse* (*Book of the Hunt*). He tells how they went ahead of their master, flushed game, and retrieved it from land or marsh.

In his 1576 treatise, *Of English Dogs: the Diversities, the Names, the Natures, and the Properties,* Dr. John Caius determines that the land spaniel should be split into two groups. There is the spring, or hawking, spaniel, which worked with a trained falcon to hunt small prey. The smaller cocking, or cocker, spaniel is named for woodcocks, a bird it often hunted. Spring spaniels and cocker spaniels were born into the same litters at this time.

In 1812, a pure line of English springer spaniels was bred by the Boughey family in Shropshire, England. It all started with a dog named Mop I. The family continued to breed the dogs until well into the 1930s. Across the ocean, the American Spaniel Club was founded in 1881. But it wasn't until 1932 that the American Kennel Club arrived at its current standards for the breed.

For more on the history of the springer spaniel, go to:

- essfta.org/english-springers/spaniel-manual /a-short-history-of-english-springer-spaniels/
  For some nifty historical paintings, check out:
- englishspringer.org/breed-history.php

The Springer Spaniel Today

The springer spaniel is a medium-sized dog that is liver color (dark brown) with white markings or black with white markings. Some have a third color, tan. They are a compact build with a proud bearing and measure between nineteen and twenty

Modern-day springer spaniel

inches in height and weigh between forty and fifty pounds. The two types of the breed are working— or field—and showing. Field-bred dogs have a shorter coat and less droopy ears.

Show dogs are bred for looks and grace of movement. As they have been for centuries, field dogs work as a hunting partner with their owner.

Their job is to move ahead of the hunter, never venturing beyond his firing range, and to flush birds from the bushes and reeds. The birds fly up, and the hunter fires. Once a bird has been shot, the springer spaniel marks with its eyes where the bird has fallen and retrieves it. The dog returns to the hunter and sits, holding the bird in its mouth without puncturing the bird's body. This "soft mouth" is the most highly prized trait of the springer spaniel.

Springer spaniels are versatile dogs. Owing to their keen sense of smell, they also make excellent "sniffer" dogs, sniffing out bombs and explosives. Other springer spaniels are trained to be rescue dogs. While they lack the hefty size of traditional snow rescue dogs—such as Barry, the legendary Saint Bernard—their keen eyesight and sense of smell make them superior all-weather trackers.

Owning an English Springer Spaniel

Springer spaniels are typically good-natured and easy to train. As with most dogs with floppy ears, they can be susceptible to ear infections without proper care. A balanced diet and a steady exercise regimen are recommended for the springer spaniel to maintain proper health and weight.

Since they are bred for both moderate undercoat and topcoat, springers shed year-round. If their coats are not well maintained, excessive shedding can occur. Regular grooming will assist in avoiding knots and mats in their coats.

If you want to find out more about this wonderful breed, visit these sites:

- essfta.org/
- springerrescue.org/

The Founding of Plymouth

In September 1620, after several mishaps, false starts, and leaky hulls, 102 colonists set sail aboard the *Mayflower* from the port of Plymouth in England. They were headed for the Virginia Colony—controlled by the Virginia Company of London—which, in those days, extended as far north as Long Island and as far south as Cape Fear, North Carolina. (Another group of investors, the Virginia Company of Plymouth, controlled the land between Maryland and Maine.) The colonists' destination was the mouth of the Hudson River in what is now lower New York State, part of the London Company's territory. The merchant investors paid for the trip in exchange for the colonists sending back furs, lumber, and other prizes of the New World. While today we call these colonists

Pilgrims, they did not refer to themselves as such at the time. Half of the passengers aboard the *Mayflower* were Saints or Separatists, so-called because they had separated themselves from the Church of England. Considered to be outlaws, they wanted to come to America to have the freedom to worship as they chose. The other half of the passengers were servants, craftsmen, soldiers, and adventurers bent on starting new lives in a new place. The Separatists called these other people Strangers.

During the sixty-six-day voyage, the passengers of the *Mayflower* suffered terrible seasickness and punishing storms. Drifting off course, the *Mayflower* landed in Cape Cod, part of the Plymouth Company's territory, instead of the mouth of the Hudson River. They immediately headed south to find their intended landing place, but the coastal waters were so brutal that they fled back north to what today is known as Provincetown Harbor. Winter was setting in—so their captain, Master Jones, told them—and here was as good a place as any to make their new home. Since their patent specified London Company land, that patent was no longer valid. Some of the passengers threatened to go south on their own. Before they went ashore in a longboat, the adult males on board met in the captain's cabin and came up with what became known as the Mayflower Compact, the agreement by which all members of the colony would live and govern themselves in the new world.

The men, under the leadership of Myles Standish, spent a month exploring the Cape Cod coastline in search of a good site for their settlement. They caught fleeting glimpses of native people, who ran away before they could make contact. They discovered the remains of old forts, dug up graves, and uncovered a buried stash of corn, which they looted. Some of the Nauset Wampanoag also attacked them, but no one was hurt, and the native men ran away. Then the colonists ventured in their newly assembled shallop—a small boat with a sail—farther up the coast in search of what one of the sailors called Thievish Harbor, said to be a hospitable place in spite of its name. There they found more graves and abandoned native houses.

On December 11, the colonists found a hillside overlooking a shallow harbor with fresh water, cleared fields, and no sign of Indian habitation. On charts made by a previous explorer, it was called New Plymouth. Here they made a plan for nineteen private houses, a common house, a storage building, and a platform for cannons. On Christmas Day, the common house was completed.

In mid-March, most of the houses were built

and the colonists were undergoing military drills when a native man walked into the settlement and welcomed the colonists in their own language. He said his name was Samoset, an Abenaki from an island off the coast of Maine. He ate and stayed overnight in the Hopkins house, went away the next morning, and came back a few days later with Tisquantum, or Squanto, and Massasoit, a Wampanoag leader from several miles away. Squanto spoke fluent English because he had been kidnapped by English explorers and sold to the Spaniards as a slave. He was rescued by Spanish friars and went to England, where he lived for several years before returning to Cape Cod. The colonists signed a treaty of friendship with Massasoit, who sent Squanto to live with them.

Squanto moved in with the colonists and became their interpreter and advisor. He showed them how to fish and how to plant Indian corn in mounds using herring for fertilizer. When the very first harvest was reaped in the fall, Governor Bradford called for a harvest feast. The Wampanoag arrived with five freshly slain deer to add to the game fowl, fish, clams, and lobster already on hand. After long months of sickness and hard work, it was a heartfelt celebration of the earth's bounty.

Much of what we know about the founding of the Plymouth settlement comes from a firsthand report called *Mourt's Relation, A Relation or Journal of the Beginning and Proceedings of the English Plantation Settled at Plimoth*. Edward Winslow wrote it, with some help from Governor William Bradford.

From this account, we know that, in addition to the 102 passengers and thirty-one crewmembers aboard the *Mayflower*, there were also two dogs. One was a male English springer spaniel, and the other was a female mastiff, both said to be the property of John Goodman. Since the dogs remain nameless in the otherwise detailed account, we can only imagine what their names might have been. It is also safe to assume that, like everyone else who made the voyage, the dogs were expected to work to earn their keep. The springer spaniel's job was to flush and retrieve game birds. The mastiff, owing to her fearsome size, served as a guard dog. We also know that there were at least thirty children on board, including Love and Wrestling Brewster (ages six and nine), Remember Allerton (five years old), and Francis and John Billington (ages fourteen and eighteen).

First published in 1622 by a Separatist known as George Mourt, *Mourt's Relation* was meant to offer a rosy picture of life in the New World to encourage more colonists to come to America.

Bright as the picture may have been intended, the overall effect to the modern reader is of a small, terrified band setting foot on a wild and inhospitable shore, where winter was closing in and the woods were filled with strange and alien noises. Was it possible that these two dogs, in addition to doing their jobs as flusher of game and watchdog, also offered comfort to the colonists?

For more information about the voyage of the *Mayflower* and the founding of the Plymouth Settlement, go to:

- mayflowerhistory.com
- plimoth.org

To see a copy of *Mourt's Relation,* check out books.google.com/books and search for "Mourt's Relation."

31901064974597